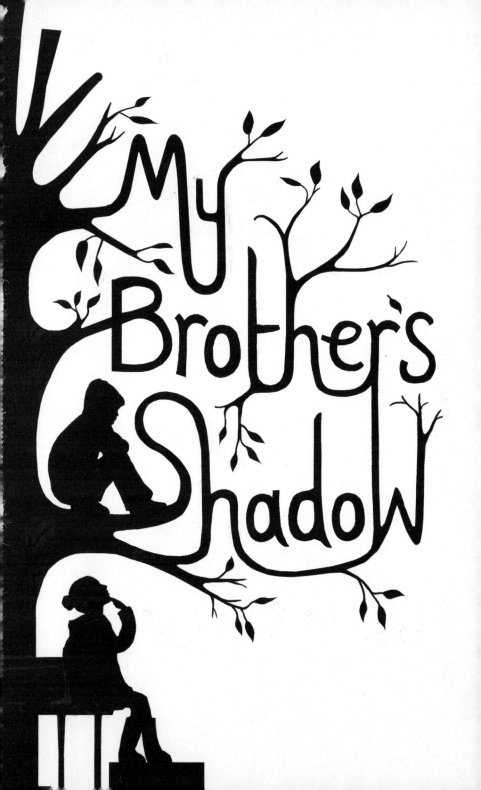

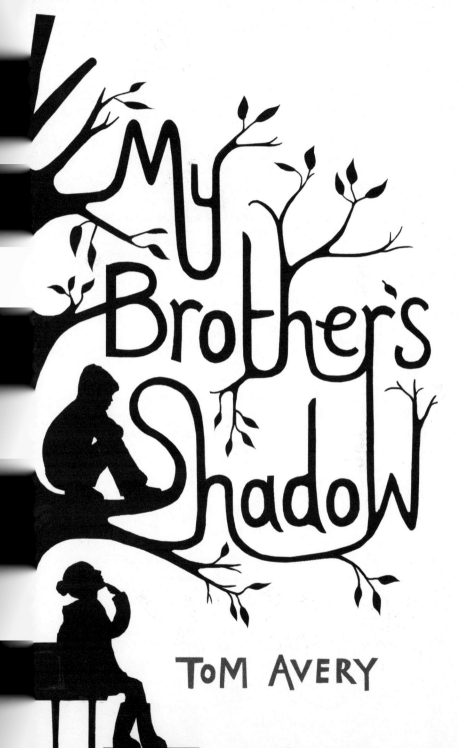

My Brother's Shadow

TOM AVERY

schwartz & wade books · new york

Text copyright © 2014 by Tom Avery
Jacket art copyright © 2014 by Kate Grove

All rights reserved. Published in the United States by Schwartz & Wade Books, an imprint of Random House Children's Books, a division of Random House LLC, a Penguin Random House Company, New York. Originally published in paperback in different form by Andersen Press Limited, London, in 2014.

Schwartz & Wade Books and the colophon are trademarks of Random House LLC.

Visit us on the Web! randomhouse.com/kids

Educators and librarians, for a variety of teaching tools, visit us at RHTeachersLibrarians.com

Library of Congress Cataloging-in-Publication Data
Avery, Tom.
My brother's shadow / Tom Avery. — First edition.
pages cm
"Originally published in paperback by Andersen Press Limited, London, in 2014."
Summary: Eleven-year-old Kaia, who has felt emotionally isolated since her brother's suicide, befriends a wild boy who mysteriously appears at her London school, finding a way to communicate with him despite his being mute.
ISBN 978-0-385-38487-2 (hc) — ISBN 978-0-385-38489-6 (ebook) — ISBN 978-0-385-38488-9 (glb)
[1. Friendship—Fiction. 2. Grief—Fiction. 3. Single-parent families—Fiction. 4. Mutism—Fiction. 5. Suicide—Fiction. 6. London (England)—Fiction. 7. England—Fiction.] I. Title.
PZ7.A9527My 2014
[Fic]—dc23
2013030321

The text of this book is set in 12-point Belen.

Printed in the United States of America

10 9 8 7 6 5 4 3 2 1

First American Edition

To the thirty wonderful children of 6TA 2011–12,
who met and loved Kaia before anyone else

ARRIVAL

It was winter when he arrived. The chill wind blew through his ragged clothes, turning his skin a raw pink. Chapped lips and bloodied gums, his face pressed against the window.

When I saw him that first time I screamed— a small and silent scream, all inside, in my gut. It was the most terrifying, the most thrilling, the strangest thing to happen in a maths lesson in a long time.

The boy dipped below the frame like a duck. He soon resurfaced.

His eyes—a sharp, cold gray—searched the classroom, passing from face to face. I stared right back.

When his eyes met mine through the frosted glass and my heart was stilled in my chest, I thought perhaps, for just a moment, a flickering smile parted those cracked lips.

Smiles can be small, tiny even, minute. Smiles can be just in your eyes. Magic, secret smiles that you don't want anyone to see but you can't help. Or magic, secret smiles that you want just one person to see—the one person you love the most, who knows your face the best.

Later, even when I knew that face, after hours and hours of staring at that furrowed brow and those thick charcoal eyebrows, hours of afternoons shared, I still wasn't sure if in that first glance there'd been a smile.

That face was the biggest mystery of all.

FROZEN GIRL

Last term Mr. Wills gave us each a yellow note-
book filled with empty gray pages.

"This is your holiday homework," he said.
"You're to write a diary of everything you do over
the break."

I didn't write anything. Well, what was I going
to write?

Monday
Mum went to work. I was meant to be going to the
holiday club at school. Instead I made a sandwich,
went to the big park and sat under an oak tree
(*Quercus robur*).

Tuesday

Mum was "sick" and didn't go to work. Heard her boss shouting at her down the phone. Think Mum's lost her job.

My mum from before would never have acted this way. My mum from before loved her job. My mum from before loved me.

I made a sandwich, went to the park and sat under a different tree, silver birch today (*Betula pendula*—the best name of any tree).

Wednesday

Mum "sicker." I stayed at home so she didn't hurt herself. Hoped she didn't hurt me.

No, I didn't write anything. But then the boy appeared. So I decided to fill these empty pages. I had something in my life to write about and someone in my life to write about.

* * *

I think they tried to take the boy away. The police probably, social workers, the teachers. They all tried to get him to leave. He screamed and barked, yelled and growled. I heard him from the classroom, where I shivered and glanced at the window. Mr. Wills set us reading to do.

I used to love books—each one a mystery waiting to be uncovered.

Long, long ago, back when no one called me *idiot* or *freak*, I used to read books just like the other girls. Now they read big fat books with thousands and thousands of words, big fat books with big fat mysteries and pretty pink covers. I still read the same books, the same books as a year ago, when I was ten, when everything stopped, not just my reading.

I'm frozen in the past. I'm frozen in a day which I'll never forget. Frozen. Frozen. Frozen. How do you defrost yourself from something you cannot see? How can you change what's happened?

I Kaia am forever frozen.

Forever frozen Kaia I am.

I forever Kaia am frozen.

So I'm not reading. I don't want to remember. Instead I'm writing this.

In the end, I don't think they could make the boy go. His wails and wild shouts must have stopped the whole school from working, so they let him stay.

At the end of the day, when Mr. Wills had given us our homework—yes, more homework— and we'd finished our daily scramble for bags and coats and empty lunch boxes, we lined up as usual outside the library. And there he was, perched like a blackbird, his knees pulled up to his chest and his toes curled around the lip of a chair amongst the bookshelves.

He stared at us again. Dev and his stupid friends made stupid jokes about his dirty, raggedy clothes.

"They're definitely from Oxfam, mate," Dev said.

Poppy, Hanaiya and all the other girls giggled. I stared right back at the boy.

It's rude to stare. That's what I've been told. But I don't know why; sometimes it's not. We're told to keep our eyes on our writing and focus on those maths problems. When I gaze at the sky or lose myself looking up through the branches of trees trying to see some pattern or order, no one tells me off. But if I stare at a person, an amazing, unique, miraculous person, I'm being rude.

We should be allowed to stare at everybody. We should be made to stare at everybody. All these incredible people and we're not allowed to stare. It's madness.

Have you seen them all? Well, I know you've seen them, but have you *seen* them? Scurrying here, busying there, all thinking different things, dreaming different dreams, with a different past and a different future, every single stupendous one of them.

It's good to stare. That should be the rule. That's

the kind of rule Moses made for me when I was sad or worried or sick.

"Tears let the sadness out," he said.

Or, "The future is full of possibilities."

Or, "Everyone's gotta be sick someday."

That's what he said—before. *Rules for life*, he called them.

It's good to stare.

So I stared right back. The boy stared. I stared. He stared. I stared. He stared. I stared.

"Come on!" Mr. Wills called. Everyone else had gone. It was just me, staring.

Someone in the library—who hadn't been as interesting as the boy—closed the door, and I scuttled after Mr. Wills with my own thoughts and dreams and past and future.

Rule for Life

It's good to stare.

ANGEL BROTHER

After the boy arrived I dreamed. Mum says that my brother is in heaven. If that's true, then he came down for the night.

With his hat pulled low he looked just the same as I remembered him. He looked just the same as when I found him, just the same as I see him every day. Well, apart from the wings.

"Hey, Tiny," he said.

I reached out my hand. Moses the angel stepped back. He stretched out his wings and rose into the air.

"Sorry, Tiny. Looky, no touchy," he said.

I asked him how he was, which I can see now was a stupid question.

That's often a stupid question: *How are you?*
People don't want to tell you how they really are
unless you're their brother or their sister. Even then
we don't share everything, do we? Mr. Wills was
always asking *"Are you OK?"* And I always lied.

"You're not to worry about me, Tiny Girl,"
my brother continued. "You need to worry about
yourself."

But that is all I've done for twelve months and
twenty-three days. I worry about school, about the
stupid kids calling me names and cackling like hyenas. I worry about Mum, about the drink and
about money. I worry.

When I awoke, and the world of dreams tinged
the waking one, worry still ate away at me, but
perhaps Moses the angel had lessened it just a little.

WILD BOY

The boy prowls the playground, a lion amongst the hyenas—all the chattering, cackling children. His rags have been replaced with a hodgepodge of lost property and an adult is with him, tailing him—Harry, who works with one child at a time in school. His job is to find out what is going on inside a child's brain. An impossible job.

Even with his escort, the boy looks dangerous.

I hear Dev calling him "Wild Child"—not to his face, of course, but in a whispered hush as he and his idiot friends scuttle past me.

Dev means it as an insult, I know that. But I don't think it *is* an insult. He is a child. And he is wild. What's wrong with that?

Wild animals are fierce and dangerous and free. Wild flowers are the most precious and beautiful. And wild thoughts are what make us feel alive. Like when I think about jumping on the table in the middle of Mr. Wills's maths lesson and shouting at the top of my voice, "I'm not stupid! I'm just stuck!"

I like the boy. He *is* wild. He scares all the idiots in my class; I can see them cower as he walks by. He has hair like a deep, starless night. And he likes staring, like me.

I stare at everyone. Everyone ignores me. Nearly everyone. Luzie catches my eye. She is sitting in a circle of my ex-friends. Her eyes are sad. Her lips begin to rise in a smile. I look away.

We're not allowed to take pens out to the playground, but I've been sitting writing all lunch. No one usually sees me, not even the teachers.

On bad days Poppy sees me. Today's a bad day.

She crept up behind me. "All right, freak," she whispered in my ear.

Giggles then from Poppy's idiot friends.

I didn't turn. I didn't answer.

"What you writing, freak?"

I'd closed the book. I held it tightly. I held my thoughts tightly.

"Whatever, freak," Poppy hissed. More giggles. Then I felt a tug on my hair as she pulled at my frizzy mop. Still I didn't move.

The boy sees me too.

I was sitting where I am now, where I'd stolen a sad glance from Luzie, where Poppy had tugged at my curly black hair—on my second-favorite bench. My coat was buttoned up and a long, thick scarf that Mum knitted an age ago was tied round my neck, face and head when I first spoke to him.

His prowl led him right past me.

He stared. I stared. His dark gray eyes tried to swallow me, but before they could I whispered, "I like your hair."

Another stupid thing to say.

His eyes flashed. I breathed in. He continued his prowl. I breathed out.

That was our first conversation.

Can you call that a conversation?

Of course. Both people don't have to talk, just respond. He flashed his eyes.

Mum says that I mustn't talk to myself, that I'll make myself go mad.

I think it might be too late for that.

THE DAY I WENT MAD

He said, "Bye-di-bye, Tiny," in the morning, pinching my sides, making me giggle. Then my brother left for school. His cap was tilted back, and just before he closed the door his big, bright eyes smiled at me. You know, one of those secret smiles. I smiled back.

I used to have a lovely smile; Mum always tells me that. Used to. That makes me sad. What's wrong with my smile now?

I went to school, same as normal. I did my lessons, same as normal. I laughed and played with all my friends, Luzie, Angelica, Gemma, Hanaiya, same as normal. Mr. Wills said that I was "so bright," same as normal, and that I'd be able to read any book I liked soon. I walked home with Luzie and Shadid, same as normal.

Then normal ran away.

In my memory everything is wrong. Our front door looks warped, the paint cracked and peeling. The lock sucks my key in, the mouth of some hungry monster. The key burns my skin like ice.

I open the door and call, "Mo!"

This is greeted by a silence so complete, so unearthly, that my breath freezes in my lungs. The chill spreads out around me and frost cracks under my feet as I step towards my brother's room.

"Mo!" I whisper into air so still I can see my words hang in the mist ahead of me.

I place my hand on Moses's door and push.

Then I see him, as I see him now—whether waking or sleeping—cut into my mind.

He is still and cold, lying on his back. His head is propped against the bed but that priceless smile is covered by his cap, fallen forwards. Apart from that all I can see is red—soaking into the carpet, smeared across the pages of discarded books, staining my last sight of my brother.

FITTING IN

Nobody talked about the boy, not like when an ordinary person joined our school.

Someone normal and straightforward and boring was the greatest fascination to my classmates. Someone normal would be mobbed in the playground, forced to tell every detail of their dull lives. Someone normal just fitted.

But this boy, this wild boy, he was too much, too wild, too extraordinary. He crashed into our lives. He haunted our days. And he fitted none but me.

Nobody talked about the boy, but there were whispers.

*   *   *

I'd spend a long time in the book corner, soaking in the covers of the books on the top shelf, the ones I still could not read. When Mr. Wills was busy reading with others, I'd pull them one by one from the shelves, gazing at the glossy pictures.

I was standing, staring at a picture of a boy with red hair sitting on a swing—it was a book I'd seen Luzie reading—when I heard the whisper and I knew straightaway who they were talking about: the boy.

"... just a weirdo. Wandering around, staring."

It was Poppy, but her table wasn't by the book corner. I pushed myself up on tiptoes and peered over the bookshelf.

Poppy was standing behind Dev and Deon. Luzie and Angelica took up the other chairs.

"We-ir-do." Dev rolled the word out like a cat-kin. Deon laughed.

"Shut up, Poppy," Luzie said. "Don't be so horrible. You heard what Mr. Wills said. We've got to include everyone, no matter how different they are."

"You shut up," Poppy spat back.

I didn't want to be there. I didn't want to listen. I tried to silently sneak back to my seat. I glanced at the table as I emerged, knocking the wobbly shelf; it shook and rocked on its uneven legs. Books crashed to the ground.

"What on earth is going on?" Mr. Wills yelled from his desk, where Shadid sat beside him reading a book about football.

All eyes were on me.

Poppy answered before I could. "Kaia was pushing in the book corner, sir."

"Sit down, Kaia. You too, Poppy. I don't know what either of you think you are doing," the teacher said. He returned to Shadid and the football book.

Poppy glared at me, anger in her cool blue eyes.

I looked away.

Luzie caught me, held my stare.

I walked away, back to my chair, an empty one beside it.

The wild boy prowls the playground. That's when we see him each day. I love it, love watching all the other kids.

The footballers, hampered by thick winter coats and dashing around after a stupid ball, stop and stare as the boy scuttles across the pitch, their game quite forgotten. Giggled conversations halt as he roams close by, sometimes baring his pearly yellow-white teeth. Little kids run squealing behind teachers, who squirm in their own rigid way. I love it.

He always comes past me, sitting on my first- or second-favorite bench, out of the way of traffic from the many games of tag. He always stops right by me and stares. I stare. He stares.

Then I speak. I tell him other things I like.

"I liked it when you growled at Dev," or "I like your trainers." He wore an odd pair, one white, one green, which I guessed he'd plucked from lost property.

Then he flashes his glorious gray eyes and continues his prowl.

That's until today. Today was different.

I had got myself comfortable, lunch finished, a thin book in my coat pocket, my scarf wrapped tightly. I was sitting on my favorite bench, a circular one, which hugs the base of a large sycamore (*Acer pseudoplatanus*), one of the most wonderful trees: *rough bark that peels away to reveal a pinky-brown flesh; three-pronged leaves, tinged with purple, especially when the sun gleams down through them; a majestic rounded dome, giving a feeling of safety as you rest beneath its aged boughs.*

Here I was, sitting, gazing heavenward, peering through the now leafless branches at the watery blue sky. It was a vast spider's web above, complete with giant spider—a long-abandoned nest, twigs poking out in all directions. I had been looking up for a long time when a clunk brought a yelp from my throat.

The boy had leapt up on the bench beside me and was staring with great intensity into the canopy.

"Hello," I said, breathless.

The boy slowly turned towards me.

"What's your name?" I asked.

He stared, silent.

So I tried again.

"My name's Kaia. What's yours?"

He didn't answer. He crouched beside me and turned his face to the cloudless blue again. I examined for a moment the angular shape of his face—the sharp pointed nose, the thick black eyebrows and hard, sticking-out jaw—then joined my new friend in staring at the sky.

Together we stared.

Together we stare.

SILENT CONVERSATIONS

I used to get in trouble. I wasn't trouble myself. But I was involved.

Did I like being involved? I don't know; my memory's frozen like the rest of me, frozen in that one moment. I guess I did, though.

We were silly and careless. We talked when we should have been listening and giggled when we should have been working.

"I'm fed up with this!" Mr. Wills would shout. "You've got to be more focused."

Why did I stop being involved? I don't think I had a choice. I stopped talking, couldn't talk to any of my friends after it happened, after I found my brother.

Found is a funny word, isn't it? It can mean a wonderful discovery: I found a fifty-pound note; I found my way; I found what I needed. And then we use it too for terrible discoveries: I found out my smile is no longer lovely; I found that all my friends stopped talking to me; I found my brother.

I'd hoped, when we moved to Year Six, I'd have a new teacher. Someone who saw me, who gave me time. Someone to help. But Mr. Wills came with us. "To help you stay settled after a difficult year," the head teacher said.

He's OK, I guess. At least I don't get in trouble anymore. Not that kind, anyway. I'm not involved.

The teacher didn't introduce our new classmate. We all knew him already. He'd prowled and growled and snarled his way through our playtimes. One day he wasn't there and the next day he was, standing in the door to our classroom, filling my mind with a low growl.

"Hello," I whispered as Mr. Wills called the register.

The boy stared. I smiled. Gray eyes flashed.

I felt Mr. Wills's eyes on me. His brow crinkled like an autumn leaf as I looked up. *Take care of the boy,* his look said.

I nodded. I beamed. Not my biggest smile, but enough to be noticed.

"I'm glad you're happy, Kaia." Mr. Wills smiled at me, almost like he used to, then returned to the register.

From a few tables away, Dev wrinkled his nose. His look was one of confusion, fear perhaps.

The boy growled.

I grinned again.

A small whimper seemed to pass Dev's lips, but if it did, no one else noticed.

Silently I stood as Mr. Wills continued the register.

"Good afternoon, Angelica."

"Good afternoon."

"Good afternoon, Sirat."

I approached with caution, watching him as he watched me. I liked him, but he was wild.

I reached out my hand. The boy didn't move, not towards me or away. I took him by the arm. He pulled it back. I smiled and tried again. This time he followed.

"Homework," Mr. Wills called, the register complete.

The class groaned almost as one.

Still I grinned; an empty seat was filled.

FAMILY

Literacy Homework

Interview someone in your family about their job for careers week next week.

Ask them:

- *What they do during the day*
- *What led them to where they are*
- *What's the best thing about their job*
- *What's the most challenging thing about their job*

There's only one other person left in my family. So I wrote these questions for her.

• Mum, what do you do during the day now that you've lost your job?

• Is it like my day? Do you spend a lot of it thinking about Moses?

• Are you frozen like me?

• Have you "moved on" yet?

• Is there anything good left?

• Is there anything that's not a challenge?

I didn't ask her these questions. I just wrote them. I didn't ask her because we don't talk anymore. We say things, we have conversations.

"How was school?"

"Fine. What's for dinner?"

"Sorry, pizza again."

"Time for bed now."

"OK, night."

"Night."

We have conversations, but we don't talk. Not like we used to. Not like we did before. Before, our flat was filled with chatter and smells and sights.

Now it's blank, frozen like me, and gray and worn like Mum. Before, our kitchen was dusted in flour and sugar and sticky crumbs; me and Mum used to bake and Moses used to eat. Our kitchen's bare now, cupboards empty apart from jars of jam and peanut butter, tins of beans, an assortment of unused herbs and spices, and bottles filled and half filled—bottles I don't touch.

I remember laughter in our home. I remember it like a dream: you know it happened, but all the details pour away through your fingers as you try to grasp them, like the sand in an hourglass. That time has been and gone.

Ignore what I said; I still do get in trouble.

"Come on, Kaia, how are you ever going to improve if you don't do the work?"

I didn't tell Mr. Wills that I couldn't. I didn't tell him that the only family I have spends most of her time whispering into a bottle rather than talking to her daughter.

So I got in trouble. I was quite pleased. At least for that moment I wasn't invisible.

He didn't do his homework either, the boy, but can you do your homework if you don't have a home? That doesn't seem fair.

Maybe Mr. Wills agreed. He didn't tell the boy off, not like he did me.

He really was wild. While I dream of leaping on tables, he did it, howling at the ceiling. When the class cackled at one of Mr. Wills's stupid jokes, the boy looked around, perplexed, then clapped and barked out an imitation of a laugh. He tore books apart, chewed pencils, bolted in and out of the classroom.

No one knew what to make of him. I loved him.

From that first day I loved him. Not *loved*, loved. You know, I think he's brilliant.

My class is noisy. They sit and talk about TV and football and clothes. I like quiet; I like to think. I'm trying to clear my head.

The boy likes quiet too, when he's not howling. He never speaks. I've not heard a word from his mouth, not a whisper of a word.

He doesn't speak, but he does listen. He's great at listening whenever I want to talk.

"I miss my family," I told him earlier today, at break time.

He stared at me, gray eyes piercing my washed-out hazelnut.

I stared back.

"I miss them all the time, Boy," I tried again.

We were on our second-favorite bench, backs against a white-painted wall, shielded by a large, raised wooden flower bed. Jo, the school's gardener, had filled it with broad beans, onions and brussels sprouts. Not much grows in winter.

"I miss my brother most. I miss his secret smiles. I miss having someone to talk to, tell all my secrets to."

The boy continued to stare, I think, to listen. I continued to talk about my family: a father I never knew; my brother gone forever; my mum lost and frozen, just like me.

A tennis ball flew past us, followed by two charging boys.

"Do you have a family, Boy?" I asked.

I wasn't expecting an answer, but this question along with many others spun through my mind. *Where does he come from? Why is he here? Is he here to stay?*

Only one person could answer these questions, and he cannot or will not.

Rule for Life

No one can open your mouth for you.

APOLOGIES

Sitting is what we do most, me and my friend.
Sitting, staring. I talk, he listens. At least, I think
he listens.

I still tell him about my family. I've told him
more about Moses than I've told anyone before—
it's easy talking to the boy. Talking to the boy is
like talking to myself; he doesn't laugh or question
or call me a freak. I tell him about trees—their
names, seasons, colors, shapes. I tell him about
school, who's who and what's what.

"Mr. Wills doesn't like me," I said to him
today.

We were in the dinner hall. Fish fingers, chips

and peas. I had nearly finished, just a few peas resting on the end of my knife. The boy was slowly slurping his orange juice.

He put it down and looked at me, brow furrowed in an expression I was beginning to recognize.

Faces are brilliant like that. It's not just the features you recognize: the nose, the eyes, the mouth. Everyone has different expressions too: a different way of smiling, saying they're happy; a different way of saying they're sad or angry or scared; a different way of saying "Go away" or "You're very welcome" or "I don't want anything to do with you." How can a face move in so many different ways?

Here's an amazing thing too: you can copy people's expressions. Even though you can't see your own face, you can model it on someone else's.

There is only so far you can go with expressions, though; only so much you can tell with a flick of an eyebrow. You need to use words some-times.

"He thinks I'm stupid so he doesn't like me," I replied to his expression, which only deepened.

"I don't think I'm stupid either," I said. Then, in a whisper, "I'm just stuck, frozen stuck."

The boy made a noise. You could call it a grunt, but that sounds like an animal and of course he's not an animal, not quite; he's a boy. It was a noise somewhere between a cough and a word, made deep in his throat.

I looked up to see Mr. Wills walking across the hall.

The boy looked down at my peas.

I looked down at my peas.

"OK," I said with a nod.

So he did it. He chopped his hand down on the end of my knife; it flipped over, sending peas high into the air. One pea dropped on the table in front of us. One pea shot off behind a group of little kids lining up. But one pea, one pea flew true. It pinged off the side of Mr. Wills's head—a perfect shot.

My eyes widened. My stomach leapt into my throat. I nearly—nearly, mind you—wet myself.

Mr. Wills turned quickly, eyes blazing. His eyebrows rocketed downwards and I knew, just knew, that he could read the guilt all over my face.

Our expressions give us away too, don't they? They can be read. And Mr. Wills read me.

"Kaia!" he shouted. "Straight to the Red-Card Room."

Now I'm here, in the Red-Card Room, the room where you go if you're naughty. It's not too bad. Mr. Wills shouts at me. I don't defend myself. I don't want my friend to get in trouble. The head teacher makes me write apologies—to Mr. Wills, to the cook, to Harry, who was in the dinner hall.

Harry thinks he knows me. He thinks he

knows all about me. He thinks he knows all about Moses. He talks to children like me, children who are frozen and stuck, children who need to grow.

Harry shakes his head and tells me he thought I had been doing so well recently.

I don't know what he means, not quite, but when Harry's talking tears spring to my eyes.

When that was done, the apologies made, the head teacher asked if I had any homework. I said that I did. Writing in my notebook is homework. At least, it was.

It was long after the last bell rang for the end of lunch and Harry's booming voice had called all the hyenas in. I think the head teacher had forgotten about me. He nearly spilled his tea when he came into the room and found me there.

"OK, Kaia. You need to get back to class now," he said. "Make sure you apologize to Mr. Wills properly. A proper sorry, young lady."

Make sure you apologize to Mr. Wills. Properly.

When was the last time I heard that word—

sorry? When was the last time someone thought

I needed to hear it? When would I get *my* proper

apology?

I'm not a freak.

I'm not stupid.

I'm frozen.

This is what I thought about as I attacked the

stairs—the long flight up to the classroom.

Animals don't say sorry, do they? Or thank

you. Animals don't feel hurt. Animals and objects.

Maybe if I were an animal, maybe if I were

wild or maybe if I were a block of ice. Maybe if

I really were frozen, then I wouldn't feel hurt. I

wouldn't care about ex-friends and lost mothers.

I wouldn't even care about Mr. Wills. I wouldn't

need the sorrys.

But I'm not a block. I'm a me. And I do care.

Back in class, my ex-friends were reading. Big

books. Chapter books. Scary books. Pink books.

Mysteries. Histories. And one boy, a book of world records.

I stood at the door. I stared at them all. I missed my friend.

"What are you doing, Kaia?" Mr. Wills called from the computer. He sounded not angry, but close, always close to anger. Ready for one of his growls and *You're driving me mad* rants.

I heard Poppy snigger. Dev pushed his tongue into the fleshy bit beneath his bottom lip and stared at me, cross-eyed.

"Come here," Mr. Wills said. Definitely close.

"I'm sorry, sir," I whispered as I stopped meters away from his desk. I didn't want to get closer. I didn't want to feel the anger pulsating beneath his skin.

"What?" He leaned forwards. He hadn't heard me. "You've got to speak up, Kaia."

"I'm sorry," I whispered. I felt my cheeks heating, my eyes welling.

"No. For goodness' sake, come closer."

By now, I knew, no one was reading. Everyone was looking at me. Leaning forwards, like my teacher.

I inched a step towards him.

"I'm sorry," I whispered again.

He stared for a moment. With a look I couldn't read. "Fine," he replied. "Just sit down. Get a book. We are reading. Silently."

As I turned, most eyes returned to books. Most, but not all. Two piercing blue, icy blue, capped with fine blond eyebrows, still stared.

Freak, Poppy mouthed as I returned to my seat.

If I were ice I wouldn't care. So I'll be ice. Cold and unfeeling.

I thought this. I sat down. I reached under my desk, into my tray. My hand fell on a book I know so well. My hand stroked the cover. And I knew I couldn't be ice. I did not take out the book. I ran my fingers across it once more. I didn't need to get it out to see its cover—the spreading limbs of a majestic ash (*Fraxinus excelsior*).

Every schoolchild knows the ash for its fruit, more commonly known as helicopter seeds. When ready to fall, the fruit gracefully spiral downwards, dispersed widely by the wind.

I stood up silently and silently walked to the book corner. I reached silently to the shelf that houses my books, my slim, dull books. I silently took the first that came to hand. I turned silently. Then I yelped, not silently.

Poppy was standing beside me.

"Please!" Mr. Wills barked. "Silent in the book corner."

"Sorry, sir," Poppy called back sweetly. Then smiled and waited till our teacher turned back to his screen.

"He's in a right bad mood cos of you, you little freak," she hissed, the sweetness gone, all bitterness now.

I tried to pass her. I tried to move away. She shoved me into Luzie, who was reading a book with a playing card on the cover. The chair and table squeaked across the floor. Luzie yelled.

"Kaia!" Mr. Wills shouted. "What are you playing at today? Get back to your seat."

I didn't reply.

Ice.

HOBBIES

I don't know where he lives. Further than my house; I know that. He walks with me, sometimes. He runs on silent feet; then he is there beside me.

On my way home, I have my notebook clutched in my hand and all I want is to write. To stop and write a sentence. To stop and write what I did not say.

But he's there with me. We trot together. Tears run as silent as the boy's footfall. We do not speak. We walk. And I lead him, not home but to Round Park.

Me and Moses named every park near home. Reservoir Park is built on a reservoir. Big Park is big. Giant Park is giant with a huge hill and the best view of the city. The Field is a wide grassy plain. Squashed Park is just some swings and a broken seesaw sandwiched between a block of flats and a row of houses.

Round Park isn't round. Round Park has a roundabout, a fast roundabout that Moses used to spin me on endlessly, while I laughed and screamed and looked at the sky. Then I'd stumble off, falling sideways, and it was my brother's turn to laugh.

This is where I lead the boy. We sit and spin the wheel gently with our feet.

"I'm not a freak," I whisper.

The boy stays silent.

"You don't think I'm a freak, do you?"

Still the boy does not answer.

"You're my friend."

We stare for a time. Above, the clouds slowly drift. Nearby, a tiny boy, all blond hair and filthy cheeks, runs while his mum sits watching his tumbles. On the other side of the park, beyond the football pitch, a stand of horse chestnuts gently sway.

"*Aesculus hippocastanum,*" I say as they come into our ever-changing view. Even from that distance I can see the scar running down the trunk of the shortest one, the stunted one. It's a scar I know well; I've run my hand along its rough surface countless times.

I talk no more; we are friends, and friends don't need to talk. I pull a pencil from my bag and I write as the world spins.

Before we left we took a tour around the trees. I plucked two long, slender leaves, as green as green. I placed one in the boy's cool palm. The other I tucked carefully between the pages of my worn yellow book; there weren't many moments I wanted to remember, but that was one.

* * *

When I get home, Mum has a new hobby. Hobby. Do I have a hobby? Trees is a hobby, I guess. I want to plant one. I want to plant something. I have a packet of seeds in my room, hidden amongst my socks, tucked out of sight. I could plant them. But then they'd be gone. So I keep them safe, locked away, frozen.

Mum's new hobby is smashing stuff. I can hear her from the street.

Smash.

There goes a plate.

Smash.

There goes a mug.

Smash.

There goes a jar of jam.

I know I'll clear it up later when Mum sleeps. I know if I clear well enough, Mum will forget it ever happened. Till she wants some toast, of course.

I don't want to see it now. I've learned when to stay away. Instead I open the front door silently, like in class, and step lightly upstairs. And upstairs I write the rest of this.

I can hear the smashing slowing down.

Smash.

A bottle of foul-smelling drink, which sprays over every surface and drips from every broken pot and plate and jar, covering the floor.

Smash.

Another plate.

Then a different sound—Mum falling into the mess she's made.

I don't know I'm crying till my paper tears as I write. Damp paper.

Through my eyes, all is damp: my pink duvet—it needs washing; my bookshelf, filled with books I once read; my chest of drawers, decorated with flowers, hand-painted by my missing brother.

In the mirror, hanging wonky, I am damp. My black hair gathered in two frizzy bunches drips with tears. Hazelnut skin is slick.

The door creaks open. Mum comes in.

I wipe the tears from my eyes and the world is dry again.

Her words are slurred and I think she's put the destruction from her mind already.

"I'm gonna 'ave a bath, darling," she says.

I nod.

Inside I scream.

I say nothing.

From my window I can see the same swaying horse chestnuts.

Cut a tree open. Count its rings. You'll know its years.

Cut me open. What is there to count? Will my years show? Or inside is there something else?

Would you find inside me all the loss, all the pain? Would you find inside me a big, fat, book-sized mystery? Does our pain show our years?

Cut a tree, and as it grows its scar will grow with it. It does not close up. It does not heal. It gets big as the tree gets big.

My scars feel big. They feel as big as I am big. I want to grow, but will they grow with me? Will they heal up?

I freeze them here because I cannot have them any bigger. I freeze everything here.

Rule for Life

Sometimes silence is empty.

Sometimes you need words.

SCHOOL TRIP

We are meant to be going on a trip. We are traveling on the Tube, across town to the British Museum.

Every day Mr. Wills asks me if I've brought back my letter. Every day I lie.

"I've forgotten it," I say.

Truth: It got caught up in the destruction, in Mum's hobby. I can't take it back, wrinkled and smelling like it does.

Mr. Wills talks to me like I'm an idiot.

"How could you forget it again? How?"

His voice gets all whiny, like a birthing cow. I saw one on TV once.

"I don't understand, how?"

In my life I've cried a lot. You'd think my eyes would have dried out.

But then, thinking about the spoiled letter, about Mum and the drinking, about what Mr. Wills and my idiot ex-friends think of me, a single hot tear escapes my eye and blips off the end of my nose.

I can feel the boy next to me, watching. I can hear his thinking, wondering. Maybe he's never seen tears.

"Come on, Kaia," my teacher says. "Don't worry. I'll call home. We'll get it sorted out."

He did. He got it sorted out.

I arrived at school early on the day of the trip. I was excited to be going out.

Jo, the gardener, was harvesting the last of the winter vegetables. I sat quietly and watched her. She was wearing one of her fantastic colored jumpers, all different stripes and squares of brightness, pink and green, white and blue today.

"Oh! You gave me a fright, Kaia," she said when she noticed me.

"Sorry," I whispered.

She smiled a warm smile. She asked if I wanted to help. I did. Sometimes I think about being older. I think about not being frozen anymore. I think about life being very different.

In these thoughts I'm a gardener, like Jo. The sun warms me as I gently push seeds into the soft soil, bringing new life. I'd like that.

We worked quietly. I liked that too.

Jo showed me how to remove the fat, bulbous brussels, how to pull up the finished plant and throw it on the compost heap.

"You've got to get the whole plant, Kaia, the roots too. They're one of the most important parts of the plant; without them, you wouldn't get lovely vegetables like this. You've got to make sure nothing stops the roots growing; otherwise they can't feed the plant. But it's just as important that you get them up so they don't keep growing beneath the soil."

She pulled up pinky-white onions, delicate compared to the big brown monsters my mum used to cook with.

"Nearly spring, eh?" the gardener said, pointing to rows of green shooting out of the neighboring bed.

Nearly spring? I thought.

Jo read my mind, or maybe she read my face. "The daffodils are nearly here." She pointed out one green shoot, whose head was cut with a flash of yellow. "That's how we know it's spring, when the daffs say hello."

When the daffs say hello.

I long for spring, for an end to the frost, an end to the fourteen-month winter.

Me and the boy go on the trip together. You have to have a partner on school trips in case you get lost. Then you're lost together, not lost alone. So I got to go with the boy. Harry walked beside us too.

I say "I got to," but it wasn't really a choice; no one else would be my partner. We didn't care. If we'd had the choice we would have chosen each other anyway. At least, I would have chosen him and I hope he would've chosen me.

We stared and talked and listened as we walked to the Tube in the chill air. I told him about the trees we passed: a slender silver birch (*Betula pendula*), bark peeling like paper; an old elm (*Ulmus glabra*), knots in the branch, like a face, inspecting us each in turn.

The boy loved the Tube; it was definitely a first for him. I loved it too. He made me see it with fresh eyes—the rush of wind as the escalators drag you deep underground, the long tunnels that stretch away endlessly, the primal roar of metal on metal as the trains career forwards.

"What is *wrong* with you?" Poppy sneered as

we stood gleefully on the platform. I had grown used to Poppy, used to her taunts, used to her looks of disgust, used to letting her comments go unchallenged. But him, the boy, I wanted to defend.

"There's nothing wrong with us." I glared back.

"Ooh!" Poppy began, her idiot friends cackling. "The freak strikes back."

Now I'd started, I couldn't stop. Rage had risen in my chest. I stepped towards her and felt my new friend step up beside me, a low growl stirring the air.

"Call us that again," I hissed.

Poppy looked at me, looked at the boy, back at me. "Ah, forget you," she said, turning her back, long blond hair whipping.

I couldn't quite believe what had happened. But it got even more amazing.

From behind me came a soft voice, an ex-friend, Luzie.

"Don't worry, Kaia. Poppy can be a right horrible you-know-what."

I couldn't speak. Had someone just talked to me without making me feel like a squashed ant?

OK, you won't believe this either: it gets even more incredible.

At lunch, Luzie sat next to me. It almost made me cry.

This is a true story.

I remember the last time Luzie sat next to me. I almost cried that time too. It was three months and seven days after the funeral.

"I don't know what to say anymore, Kaia," she said.

I did not answer her. I had no words.

I heard her sniff and her voice crack as she spoke again. "If you want to talk to me, you can talk to me. But ..."

I didn't look at her. I heard her sniff again. Out of the corner of my eye, I saw her hand wipe across her face.

"But ... my mum says you might want to be alone for a while."

Still I was silent. I didn't nod. My eyes stared straight forwards.

Luzie stood and walked away, sniffing. Then I looked up as my last friend left.

IMPERFECTIONS

I don't want to talk about the funeral, but it happened.

Family were there. Granny and Grandpop flew all the way over; Mum's sister and my cousins came down from Coventry.

Moses's friends came too, all caps and black jackets.

They called me Tiny and I didn't answer. They hugged Mum, who stood like a tree trunk.

They weren't my brother. They weren't Mum's son.

The funeral happened on a Tuesday. I remember this because all through the service, as the vicar prayed and Mum cried and tried to say things about her son, I kept thinking that I was missing swimming at school. I should have been remembering my brother, but in my head I was doing widths.

I missed a few weeks of school, almost a month. I sat and cried with Mum, who said it was just me and her now. I sat and cried with a social worker lady, who promised she'd try to come back and visit but never did. I sat and cried with Granny, who said she was always there for me and then flew hundreds of miles away.

When I'd cried all my tears and buried the pain somewhere between my heart and my stomach, Mum sent me back to school.

At first everyone tried to be nice. My friends hugged me and held on to me, like my sadness was something they could suck out of me. I shrugged them off.

They whispered sorrys and asked if I was

OK—stupid question. They spoke of happy things. I closed my ears and kept my own thoughts locked away.

Eventually they stared at me like I was a curiosity, a puzzle that couldn't be solved.

I wasn't much to look at, and in the end they even gave up on staring. All except Luzie. She sat by me long after I was just a freak to everyone else. Her sad glances and her hopeful smiles did not cease.

I lost Moses. Luzie lost me.

It didn't all change on the school trip. It couldn't all change. Not just like that. It wasn't like Luzie talked to me all break time even. It wasn't like before. But it was something, something out of the ordinary.

Normally I'm surrounded by empty seats.

Later in the day, the boy and I stole away. I love that phrase. We didn't actually steal anything really, except some time.

So we stole away, away from the rest of the class, from Mr. Wills, from Harry, who was talking to Shadid and a group of boys about Egyptian hieroglyphics and ancient graffiti. We found ourselves in a room full of patterns: patterns on vases, patterns on tiles, patterns on boxes—beautiful, intricate patterns, shapes and flowers and vines and letters, some in a soft flowing script, some square and printed.

A man stood in front of a wall of tiles, speaking. A group of children sat in front of him, listening. We crouched behind, eavesdropping.

"Can anyone spot the mistake in this one?" the man asked, pointing out an almost-cross-shaped tile.

A girl near the front, a yellow bandanna holding her hair down, put her hand up and told him that one of the letters was missing a line.

"You see," the man went on, "most Islamic artists will add a deliberate mistake to their work to make it imperfect. They believe that only God is perfect, and they show this in their art."

We wandered on, into the gallery.

"That's like people, isn't it?" I said to the boy.

He stared back at me.

"Everyone's got something wrong. No one's perfect."

We looked at a large vase, about half as tall as me. I was searching for the mistake.

"Just, we're the only ones brave enough to admit it."

I thought this might be true, even though I felt far from brave.

The way back was much like the way there. It was much like it, the walking, the Tube. But it was also very different; I wasn't afraid of Poppy or the other girls. Luzie smiled at me and I smiled back. And I noticed as I stared at the others, my classmates, they all had things wrong, just like me.

When we got back into the playground and stood shivering, waiting for our parents, Jo was no longer by the flower beds, but a different face, just as welcome, said hello: a soft yellow star, the first daffodil.

Rule for Life

Smile—spring has sprung.

GROWING

After the school trip, my angel brother came down again.

He sat on the end of my bed. He hadn't sat before, just sort of hovered. I could see the wounds, thick streaks of red across his wrists, still glistening, wet, sticky. They made me think of jewels; rubies set in golden skin. I wondered how much a ruby that size would be worth.

He looked where I was looking and pulled his sleeves down to cover the terrible chasms.

"Hey, Tiny," he said.

I said "Hey" back.

Bright eyes glowed out from under a flat-brimmed cap. Moses cast them around the room, then fixed them back on me. "You're growing," he said.

I didn't feel like it. I hadn't had new shoes or trousers in ages, not since the last time I'd seen him in the waking world. I told him so.

"No," he said, pressing his hand against his chest. "In here, you're growing."

I placed my own hand on my own chest. Inside, my heart beat and fluttered. We sat still a long time. I felt in the darkness the pulsing warmth of my body.

"I'm growing?"

"You're growing. And it's good. You've got to grow," the angel Moses said.

Mr. Wills has been teaching us about similes and metaphors, when you compare something to something else that it's like.

Here's a famous simile by William Words-worth:

> *I wandered lonely as a cloud*
> *That floats on high o'er vales and hills*

It's good, isn't it? The cloud, lonely, wandering, high, away from everything.

When Mr. Wills told us about it I was staring out the window, inspecting the clouds, making it make sense.

"You've got to pay attention, Kaia!" he shouted at me. "This is important, you've got to focus."

I know, I thought. *And I was.* But I didn't say anything; I just stared back at the board as if that rectangle of white were where you could learn everything under the sun.

Poppy and the clever table got to write sim-ile poems about animals, describing the way they look, act, feel.

We had a "fill in the blanks" worksheet. Stupid stuff like:

The boy ran as fast as ...
A lion's mane is like ...
The teacher was as fierce as ...

I hate doing stupid work. Mr. Wills shouted at me again; he was in a bad mood. "You're just not trying."

He was right. I wasn't.

My favorite one we looked at is by Valerie Bloom, which is the most wonderful name. This one's a metaphor:

Time's a thief ... leaving you with tears and sighs.

I talked to Harry that afternoon, in the hall, outside of class. Harry was trying to watch the boy, who was circling the large room, swooping like a bird, but I wanted to talk to him.

We wrote a poem together, me and Harry. I did the talking. Harry did the writing. He let me take it and copy it out in my notebook.

NOW SHE GROWS

Out in the cold like a windblown willow,
Weeping branches pushed here and there,
Full of sorrow like water fills the sea,
She sits, she stares.

Lonely as a cloud, not like any other,
She wanders, so distant, so apart.
Like a patterned tile is her smile,
Ruined, imperfect, marred.

Time stole her happiness in a moment,
The crook, the thief,
But now she grows,
Heart grows, like roots beneath.

VOMIT AND PANCAKES

Mum was sick, really sick.

I was awakened by a crash. My eyes opened. The darkness was complete except for a narrow slit in the curtains.

From behind my door I heard a soft groan. I stayed as still as possible and listened. And listened. Another groan.

I pushed my duvet to one side; I knew that voice, my mother's.

It was just as dark in the hallway, but now that my eyes had adjusted, outlined objects became clear. My mum lay sprawled across the floor. A bottle, the neck smashed, rested just out of reach of her hand. A pool of sadness circled both my mother and the bottle; its stale tang attacked the back of my throat.

"Mum," I whispered.

The body groaned again.

I crouched, carefully avoiding the vomit.

"Mum," I whispered again, closer this time.

She turned her head and peered up at me through her waterfall of hair, matted with muck. She pushed herself up to her knees. I put my arms under her armpits—no avoiding the sick now— and heaved her into a sitting position against the wall.

She mumbled wordlessly, then breathed out, "Water."

I fetched her water. I made her drink. After she'd sat awhile, I led her into the bathroom. I gently undressed her and washed her down, then led her to her bed.

She spoke once more before sleep overcame her.

"My Kaia," she said, "it's just me and you now."

I stood above her, looking down at the wreck

that had been my mum. I stood a long time in the dark.

At last I spoke. "It's just me, Mum, not me and you. You're not here. You're even more frozen than I am."

I don't know where it all came from, probably the same place where I'd buried my pain, somewhere between my heart and my stomach, but it kept on coming.

"Things have got to change, Mum. We've got to change and grow and . . . and . . . live."

I turned. I left my snoring mum. I cleaned up her mess.

When I finally clambered into my bed, I found that tears covered my face and I knew that I had to say those words to my mum again, next time when she was awake.

I awoke to the smell of pancakes and my mother's guilt wafting under the door. I followed that smell. I love pancakes.

"Morning, darling," my mum said, her eyes still bleary but a smile hiding her shame.

I didn't smile back.

"I've made pancakes," my mum continued.

I still didn't smile.

She stopped smiling and sat down next to me.

"I'm sorry, Kai."

I rolled my eyes back and glanced at the short stack of pancakes. I love pancakes.

"I'm sorry, sweetheart."

I picked at the tablecloth. I flicked a few bread crumbs onto the floor.

"Come on, darling, talk to me."

I looked at my mum.

I didn't speak.

Timing is everything. Spring buds appear, new growth, ready for the approaching summer sun. Chicks are born, high in their lofty homes, and squirrels leave their winter beds once the last frost has departed.

Timing is everything. The day before, Mr.

Wills had handed out a *really special* letter. The first people to reply would do bike training: a whole week out of class, cycling.

Timing is everything, and I had a chance this day.

I spoke.

"OK, Mum," I said with the slightest hint of a smile.

"OK?"

"OK."

"Pancakes?"

"Pancakes," I replied with a nod. "Mum, I've got a letter needs signing."

"Of course, of course," she said, piling warm pancakes onto my plate, then glugging syrup all over them.

I love pancakes.

Rule for Life

Pancakes are like a blue sky—

they make any day a happy day.

DAYDREAM

"Have you got a bike?" Mr. Wills asked.

I had rushed into school before the other kids arrived, stuffed with pancakes. Mr. Wills was in the classroom, staring at his computer screen.

"Yes," I said. I did have a bike. Mum had bought it over a year ago, before it happened, for my birthday. Moses had bought me a big, heavy book, *Trees of Britain: An Illustrated Guide*. I loved both presents.

The bike wasn't new, but that didn't matter. Moses had painted it, pink like cherry blossoms, fixed up the broken parts, greased it, made it run. "Better than new," he said. "Special, just like you, Tiny."

I know I smiled then.

"OK," Mr. Wills went on. "Well, I'd better just check with Harry." I stared away from him. "You know he likes to work with you sometimes."

When I "worked" with Harry we made pictures, or folded paper into all sorts of shapes like birds and flowers, or wrote poems, and he asked me questions, lots of questions. I told him I was fine.

Mr. Wills said I should go back outside. I didn't. I went to the library.

I can hear the bell ringing outside as I write this. Time for school to start.

At lunch, while the boy snarls at passing children, I have a daydream.

I'm sitting on my favorite bench, Moses to my left, the boy to my right. We watch as the school starts to crumble away like a sand castle in the wind.

It starts with a deep whine, a primal squeal;

the hyenas stop their laughing and chatting and pointless ball games and stare up at the red building. The screech turns to a sigh, as if the walls have finally, exhaustedly given up. Then pieces of brick, chunks large and chunks small, trickle and tumble down the walls along with gritty white mortar. Next come the roof tiles: discolored, coated with furry green moss, they fall, landing with a shattering smash. Panes of glass along with rotted wooden frames fall forwards, disappearing in the pile of debris.

I catch sight of Mr. Wills, still inside his classroom, deep in conversation with Harry. He's shaking his head. "No, Kaia can't do cycling." Papers, tests, books, plastic calculators come streaming out of the gaping holes where windows once were.

Around me, the kids, frozen amidst the chaos, begin to turn to dust one by one. I see Poppy go, Dev, Hanaiya, Shadid. I add Luzie to the bench, next to the boy.

Finally, with a second wail, despair in its voice,

the building falls in on itself. A great cloud of dust rises into the air. We shield our eyes.

When it settles we're all that's left: us and the tree against our backs.

I laugh, not at the destruction, at the freedom.

PROPER ARTIST

Today, the day of the pancakes and handing in the all-important letter, Harry asked Mr. Wills if some pupils could come out and help with a "special" project.

"Who would like to go and work with Harry?" Mr. Wills asked.

A funny thing in my class—maybe it's the same in all classes—but whatever the task, no matter how dull, if a teacher offers a job, most of us would bite his hand off to do it.

So my finger was not the only one pointing to the heavens, but it was certainly the first.

"Go on then, Kaia," my teacher said. "And ...

and ..." He glanced from eager face to eager face. "And Shadid."

I leapt to my feet, almost like the boy would have, and saw Shadid, an ex-friend, smiling across the room. We headed for the door, where gray eyes in the boy's wild face waited to greet us.

The "special" project, it turned out, was more fun than I could have guessed. Harry wasn't just a man who worked with wild boys and sometimes-frozen girls like me. When school ended, Harry was an artist, a graffiti artist. I know, that's almost too cool, isn't it?

The head teacher asked Harry, with the help of some pupils—the boy, me and Shadid—to paint a small wall in the playground. I told you, far more fun than I could have guessed.

We started by thinking of ideas. What did school mean to us?

HARRY

1. Fun

2. Learning

3. Possibility

SHADID

1. Friends

2. Football

3. Making us better at stuff

Harry asked if he could change that last one to learning too. Shadid wasn't so sure.

THE BOY

. . .

KAIA

1. Trying to move on

2. Trying to change

3. Trying to escape

Harry wanted us to draw some images that showed what we meant so he could take them away and design the wall based on our pictures. He rolled out a long sheet of paper like wallpaper—maybe it *was* wallpaper—and we drew all over it.

Shadid, obviously, drew footballs and footballers, standing and running and kicking. Harry drew a big brain with things like sums and words and paintbrushes going into it, and things like money and people doing jobs and medals coming out of it. The boy, with a little help from me, drew trains and trees and children sitting.

I thought for a while, after I'd got the boy started. Harry let me think as long as I needed. I needed a long time. I wished Mr. Wills would just let me think sometimes. Then I drew a building falling down, collapsing, bricks everywhere. I drew children turning into birds, free. I drew bird-children flying high in the sky. I drew wild birds swooping and gliding. I drew baby birds be-

ing sheltered under a bigger bird's wing. I drew
and drew and drew.

When we finished and the wallpaper was
covered with our scribbling, we walked round it,
looking down at all the pictures.

Shadid stood by my drawings, staring. I knew
what was coming. I knew they were rubbish. I
knew Shadid would be telling everyone about the
stupid pictures I'd drawn.

"Harry," he began. I waited for the stinging
words. "These are brilliant, aren't they?"

I nearly choked. I could feel my face burning,
my heart beating.

Harry was next to him now. "You know,
Shadid," he replied, "they really are."

Shadid looked up at me. In his eyes there was
no laughter, cruel and cold, no shades of an insult,
nothing but friendship. "You're like a proper artist,
Kaia."

I looked down at my own pictures. I looked

at the boy's. He was still scribbling. I looked at Shadid's.

"They mean so much, Kaia. That's what makes them special," Harry said. "I can see that they mean so much to you."

I was smiling now, though my heart still beat at my chest and my face must have been a bright red.

"That's what makes great art, Kaia," Harry went on. "When it means something, when you know that it means something important and deep to the artist."

Then Shadid did something that I don't think anyone had done for a very long time. He touched me. I didn't touch him, like picking up my mum and getting her to bed. It wasn't an accident, fingertips brushing against my hand as a pen is passed. It wasn't just a bustled queue, lining up for lunch, or a push, or kick, or tug of my hair from Poppy or her friends.

He reached up and clapped his hand to my shoulder.

"I'll have to tell everyone about our secret artist," he said.

I want to tell Mum all about the art, my art. I want to tell her how fun it was. I want to tell her and I want her to be proud.

But I can't. We don't talk. So I write it here, in my room. I write it and it seems even more real, but somehow even more unbelievable too.

Today is Thursday. Thursday is Special Achievement Day. Special Achievement Day is when one child from every class gets called out in assembly and their teacher tells everyone why they've been special. I haven't been Special Achiever since before, before I found my brother. Sorry, that should be *I hadn't*.

I sat with my class, lined up on benches. We

sit in register order. I'm last, at the very end of the bench.

All the other classes go before us, because we're the oldest. Then the head teacher said, "I think we have a *very* special achiever from Year Six. Mr. Wills?"

And then Mr. Wills started speaking: "I'm giving the award this week to someone very special, someone who's been making a lot of effort to make new friends recently, and now, to try new things. Yesterday this person impressed Harry so much"—Harry smiled at this—"that he rushed into my classroom at the end of the day telling me that this *artist*"—and he said that word really long and loud—"must be Special Achiever today, and I agree. All this pupil needs to do is concentrate a little more, focus, be a bit more involved, and I'm sure she'll be Special Achiever again soon." Then Mr. Wills looked at the class and said, "Our Special Achiever this week is ..."

"KAIA!" my whole class screamed together. I

could hear Shadid screaming loudest and I knew he must have told everyone, like he said.

I walked to the front as they clapped. Not everyone clapped. I could see Poppy and some of her friends, arms crossed in the back row. Dev made a stupid face like he was clapping as a joke. But the boy's eyes were bright, secret-smile bright, and Luzie was beaming and Shadid was kneeling up on his bench.

I felt sick. I don't know why. But I felt sick. And as the head teacher handed me my certificate and shook my hand, I felt even sicker and I shook all over.

So I turned and ran out of assembly, straight into the toilets, and was sick.

PANGRAMS AND ALGEBRA

I'm trying to concentrate.

It's been days since I handed in my bike-training letter and Mr. Wills has told us nothing. Lots of the others keep asking who gets to do it. I haven't asked.

I'm trying to concentrate on what we're learning. I'm trying to be involved again. So to show I've been concentrating:

A pangram is a sentence which contains all the letters of the alphabet. A perfect pangram wouldn't repeat any of the letters either, but that's almost impossible. There's a famous one, the one Mr. Wills told us about first. Here it is: *The quick brown fox jumps over the lazy dog.*

It's nice. Mr. Wills says we're not to use the word *nice*. He says there's always a better word. But he's wrong. Sometimes *nice* is the best word. Sometimes it's exactly the right word. Sometimes the thing you want to describe is nice; it's not more or less than that. It's nice. That pangram is nice. It's not funny, or clever, or interesting. But it is nice.

Mr. Wills wanted us to make one of our own. It's much more difficult than you imagine.

We've been learning about algebra too.

Algebra is a kind of maths where unknown numbers are represented by letters. They're called variables. Like when you have to work out the area of a rectangle, $a = l \times w$, where a = the area, l = length and w = width. The width and the length can change, they're the variables, and then you get a different area, a different outcome.

Is it hurting your brain? It hurts mine.

Here's my other way of explaining it: $B = x + y + z$.

B = the boy; x, y and z are all the things that

have happened to him, all the things that have made him who he is; a boy without words, a boy without a home, a wild boy.

Here's my attempt to sum up everything we've been learning.

Kaia White lives in a hazy, jagged dream because of x, p *and* q.

Where x is what Moses did, p is how my mum has changed and q is everyone else.

Rule for Life

Pay attention—you might miss something.

TEARS AND LAUGHTER

We found out the all-important news. We found out today. We found out who gets to cycle.

Nothing else really matters from the day. We did maths, sequences, not too hard. We did literacy, writing reports; we had to write fictional reports on a pretend *really cool* new trainer—I don't care about trainers, especially not *really cool* imaginary ones. But I'm trying. I'm still trying. We did some science—upthrust is a force that makes objects lighter in water. I'm still concentrating.

Then at the end of the day Mr. Wills said, "I've just got a few letters to hand out." The class all started whispering at once. Like cows that lie down, knowing it's going to rain, we knew what was coming. We just knew.

Mr. Wills walked between the tables, making his way to each person in turn, calling out their name.

"Shadid," he said first of all, handing a beaming Shadid his letter. Everyone at his table craned to read it at once.

"Deon" next.

"Yes!" Deon squealed, then grinned across the room at Shadid. Everyone else's groans were ignored.

"Luzie." That made me smile; in my book she deserved it.

When Mr. Wills was halfway round the class he looked up, peering from table to table. "Where's Angelica?" he asked with a huff.

"You sent her to ask the office something, sir."

"Oh, yes, I did."

Mr. Wills had nearly completed his circuit of

the classroom, a classroom mostly full of disappointed faces. Just our table left. I felt sick. Again. I could feel eyes, jealous eyes, creeping all over me.

"Last but not least," the teacher said, "here you go." Then he smiled at me and the boy. "You deserve it," he said, and handed us a letter of our own.

"Oi, freak," a voice called as we walked across the playground, leaving school.

I glanced backwards. Poppy was following. My feet stumbled as my brain decided whether to stop or not. The boy steadied me with an arm.

"That should be me cycling," Poppy growled as her friends poured in behind her.

My feet continued forwards while my eyes continued to look behind. I felt her step round me, but I did not know what she planned.

"Hi, Poppy," Luzie said, her voice high and jolly, like a warbling bird. She stood in front of me.

"Move," Poppy spat, trying to step around my ex-friend.

"Hi, Poppy," Angelica sang, running up beside Luzie.

"I said move."

Luzie turned and smiled at me.

The boy's hand was on my arm. He pulled me towards the gate. As we jogged away I glanced back once more—Poppy glared at me past a wall of my friends.

I floated home. I didn't really float, but I felt like it, my feet meters above the ground. I was so excited to be picked, so excited that Luzie and the boy were doing it too. And, I guess, Shadid as well.

Then I got home. Then I got home.

Usually when I get home the flat is empty, empty and cold. I put my stuff away. I watch some TV. Mum stumbles in. We have some food. I go to bed. Mum drinks.

Today Mum was sitting in the living room, TV off, not a bottle in sight. I could hear her in there as soon as I got in. She was crying.

I hung up my bag quietly, took off my shoes and listened as she blew her nose and tried to end her tears. I didn't know whether to go in or not, to check if she was OK, to comfort her. Like I said, we don't really talk, me and Mum. She decided for me.

"Can you come in here, Kaia, please?" she called, her voice all high and squeaky.

I went in, wriggling my cold toes; the sun was out, but it didn't seem to be able to warm the world enough. Mum was clutching a piece of paper; it had been folded but was now flat. I could see several gold stickers across the top and I knew what it said:

For outstanding achievement in Art and making real effort to try new things and make new friends. Kaia White—Special Achiever

"Why didn't you show this to me, Kaia?" Fresh tears bloomed in my mum's eyes as she spoke.

I stared at her. I didn't say anything. I didn't say, "You haven't shown any interest in me for over a year. Why would I show you this?" I didn't say anything.

"Has it been that bad, love? Have I been that bad?" my mum asked.

I stared and still didn't speak. I didn't say, "The only times that haven't been bad are when I've been with a boy who can't even speak." I didn't say anything.

"I'm so sorry, darling!" Then my mum started crying properly, full-blown wailing, her head in her hands.

I didn't say anything.

I walked over and sat down next to her. I took the certificate out of her hands. "This is a good thing, Mum," I said.

She made a funny snorting sound like a pig

laughing and looked up. "I know," she said. "I know, petal."

You can sit with someone for a long time in silence, can't you? Just sitting and thinking your own thoughts but with someone, someone who's thinking their own thoughts too. Sometimes, sometimes you have the same thought. Me and Mum did. We had exactly the same thought.

"Come on." My mum took me by the hand and led me into the kitchen. She opened up cupboards, one after the other. From each she pulled a bottle, some small, some large. Each one she opened and emptied, pouring the entire contents down the sink.

We were smiling when she started. We were laughing by the end.

MAGNETS

Still he has not spoken. Not a peep, not a sound, not a whisper. He makes lots of noises and gestures and expressions, but no speaking.

It's not starting to bother me. He couldn't bother me—he's my best, best friend. That sounds stupid, I know, but he is in all the important ways. I can tell him anything. I can rely on him to stick up for me. He's changed everything.

So it's not starting to bother me, but I do at times find myself longing for more, more response than a flash of gray or a gentle laugh, or a leaf plucked from a low-hanging branch and handed to me.

Today we sat, backs against a solid trunk on

our favorite bench. I had told him all about Mum, about our new start, about the special group she says she's going to tonight, a group to help people who drink too much. This is big stuff I'm telling the boy; big, important stuff.

He watches, listens, eyebrows moving, dark against his pale skin, eyes flashing at all the right moments. When I'm done he stares into the tree above, looking for the nest we spotted a few days before—a nest, we think, containing newborn chicks.

I don't know about birds. I know about trees, I know all about trees, but not birds. So when he nudges me and points up, I don't know what bird flies in with a worm wriggling in its beak, a mother feeding its babies.

We sit together and stare above.

"Hey, daydreamer," a voice says.

We rejoin the world and find Luzie standing in front of us. Luzie and Angelica.

"You wanna play a game?" Luzie asks. And I

do, I want to play a game. I want to play a game with other people. I want to play a game.

The game we play involves magnets, which, until someone convinces me otherwise, I believe are magic. Well, they are, aren't they? How do you get two things that are not sticky to stick to each other? Magic. How can you drag one piece of metal around by another piece of metal without attaching them in any way? Magic. How can you push something away without even touching it? Magic.

So the game involved magnets. Luzie's got all these magnets that look like little pebbles. You have to place them on the lines of a special felt board without letting any two magnets touch each other. That sounds entirely dull. It's not.

We played all break time. I played all break time. I played all break time with my friends.

PAPIER-MÂCHÉ

My brother casts a long shadow; thawing is a slow process.

Slowly, slowly, rays of warmth were breaking through and moments of happiness were cracking the ice.

My tears had frozen. My laughter had too. But last night was the first time I'd laughed since before. My laughter is beginning to thaw but my tears already have.

Tears are strange. Strange because we have sad tears and happy tears, but they're always when the world is too much to bear, an overflow of our emotions, our joy and our sorrow leaking out.

I'd love some happy tears.

It was Art today. Always Art on Friday afternoons. We were making models of fruit. I'm not sure why. We'd already made wire frames; we've been working on them for weeks. Now it was time to cover them.

Papier-mâché. Have you ever done papier-mâché? It's brilliant. Simple and brilliant. You turn soft, bendable, rippable paper into something hard. Some people had to go round school asking all the classes if they had any old newspapers. Some people had to mix up the glue with a bit of water to make a paste. The others, me included, read and waited.

The boy was in class today and in my group. Me, the boy, Luzie and Gemma. We had to have groups to share the pots of paste. School's strange like that. Groups and lines and classes and partners and teams. Does the rest of the world work like that? I guess it might. Can't we just be me and you and him and her, each ourselves, each one of us "me" and no one else?

I think the boy reads. I know he won't or can't talk. But he listens, he understands. He responds with a flash of his deep pools of magnificent gray. Does he read? I think so.

He stared intently at a book on forests and jungles. I thought for a moment, while he stared at the page, maybe that's where he's from, like Mowgli in *The Jungle Book*. But then I remembered his rags, not fur and vines, but ragged old clothes. He didn't get those in no jungle. And besides, there isn't a jungle near my school.

When the newspaper was gathered and the paste was mixed, we all got our frames. Mine's a banana; the boy's is a banana too. Poppy and Hanaiya handed out the newspaper. Dev snatched a whole stack from them and started quickly tearing little shreds, dipping them in the paste, then sticking them hurriedly to his ... apple? ... orange? ... I'm not sure.

Poppy'd nearly reached my table when she stopped.

"Well, what's this then?" she said, holding up a sheet of old and crumpled news, the rest cascading to the floor, feathers drifting out of the sky.

Mr. Wills looked up from where he was working, helping someone who wasn't in on the day we made the frames. "What is it, Poppy?"

"'Gang Member Found Dead,'" she started to read.

I froze again. I froze. And I'm back, the cold air chilling me, frosted carpet crunching underfoot.

"'Police are investigating the suspicious death of a teenage boy . . . ,'" Poppy intoned.

I step towards his room, Moses's room, listening to the silence.

"'. . . found by family members yesterday afternoon.'"

I reach out. My hand pushes the door. It slowly creaks open.

"'The investigating officer'"—a face flashes in my mind: mustached, wide-mouthed Inspector Runcorn; questions run through my head, questions he asked in hours and hours of interview—"'has stated that no possibilities are being ruled out at this stage of the inquiries.'"

The door's wide open now and there he is lying as I found him, cap forwards, a mess of blood.

"'MOSES WHITE'S FAMILY'"—and she said this in capitals—"'continues to be questioned as to the circumstances surrounding his death.'"

A mess of blood and a shadow reaching out, casting itself over my life, my brother's shadow.

"POPPY!" Mr. Wills roared, halting the reading and breaking the spell. "Stop that this instant!"

I leapt up. I ran, pushing past Poppy, through the door, and once again threw up in the girls' toilets.

I didn't go back into class. No one tried to make me. I sat alone in a cubicle.

A hesitant knocking. A quiet voice.

"Kai."

I stayed silent.

"Kai, it's all right—Poppy's an idiot," Luzie said.

Still my mouth stayed shut.

Rustling and the sound of hands slapping down on the cold floor; then Luzie's face appeared at the bottom of the door. She was lying down. She stared at me. I stared.

"Kai, do you wanna talk to me?"

A single tear appeared.

"Or Harry's waiting outside."

No one made me go back to class. And no one could make me talk.

Thawing is a slow process, especially if someone sticks you back in the freezer. No one could break the ice now. No one but me.

CUP OF TEA

Floating in through my window, he came again. It's funny that he floats; he has wings but he doesn't use them.

The wounds in his arms had broken open. Thick, dark blood dripped down, dousing my duvet in a flow of red. I didn't mind; it was warm, it was Moses.

I just stared for a long time. Rivulets of blood crept under the duvet, washing against my skin, soaking into my too-short pajamas.

"Tiny?" he said after long minutes, hours, days, weeks of staring.

I nodded. A small nod, my head left hanging on my chest, too heavy to rise again.

"My tiny girl."

I nodded the same nod, shaking warm salty tears I didn't know were there from the end of my nose. Tears and blood mingled in a familial sea of sorrow, washing across my bed.

It's too much, I thought.

"It's too much," I said.

Quiet again, I watched the blood swirl as I shifted my legs.

"Tiny," Moses the angel said, drawing my eyes away from the bloody bed and up to his face. Smiling eyes pierced. "It *is* too much."

I continued to stare.

"That's why you've got to let me go."

"Let you go?"

"Let me go. You're ready." Moses whispered the last two words.

"I'm ready," I said.

Before Moses was an angel, Mum woke me up every morning, a cup of tea in hand. Every morning, mind you. She hasn't made me a tea in bed since that day.

And then, this morning, Saturday, tea. Its steam rose from the windowsill like snakes disappearing into undergrowth. And my mum sat at the end of the bed in the same place, exactly the same place where Moses had sat the night before.

"Morning, my sweet," Mum said.

She smiled at me. I smiled back. She handed me my tea. I took a sip. She'd forgotten that I like sugar. I didn't tell her.

I hadn't told her about the day before either, about Poppy and the old newspaper. I didn't tell her now. I didn't tell her about Moses.

"I've got some good news, Kai," she said.

I nodded, taking another sip.

"They've got me a job interview, the job center."

I nodded again.

"Nothing big, I might not get it, but ... but I wanted you to know I'm trying, petal."

"Thanks, Mum," I said.

She smiled. I smiled. She got up, smoothing down the duvet covering my legs, took several paces towards the door, then stopped as if she'd just remembered something.

"Have you got any homework?" she asked. That's another thing she hasn't done since before.

She really is trying.

"Let her keep it up," I whispered as she left.

Rule for Life

Memories are like a cup of tea—

don't hold them too tight.

FAVORITE BOOK

Literacy Homework

Write a review of your favorite book. Make sure you include:

- *What makes it your favorite book*
- *A synopsis of the whole story*
- *A description of a character*
- *Who you would recommend the book to*
- *Don't give too much away, though!*

I will do this homework. I will do this homework because I already have a favorite book. I already have a favorite book and I want to talk about it. It's time to talk about it. It's time to let go. I'm ready.

But what if people laugh? What if everything goes backwards? What if Shadid and Luzie and even the boy think I'm mad? Because I am mad.

No, the boy won't think I'm mad. And everyone else . . .

I'll give them all a chance. I'll be involved. I'll be me. For the first time in forever and forever I'll just be me and I'll say what's inside. Everything that's inside.

Trees of Britain: An Illustrated Guide

My favorite book is not a story, even though I love stories. I love stories much, much more than information books, much, much more. I love the mystery, the plot unfolding, developing in your mind. I love all the characters, good and bad, almost-real people who leap off the page and walk around in your world. I love escaping in a story. But I can't talk about a story, because none of them are my favorite book. My favorite book is *Trees of Britain: An Illustrated Guide.*

What makes this my favorite book?— This is my favorite book because it's the last thing that my brother ever gave me. If that's not a reason for a favorite book, I don't know what is.

A synopsis of the whole story—The whole story? This book doesn't have a story. Well, that's not true, is it? The words in this book don't tell a story. But the story of the book, well . . . Moses died on the 13th December, fifteen months and seven days ago. My birthday is on the 18th November. Moses gave me this book almost a month before he left. Every day he asked me if I was enjoying the book. I lied. I said that I loved it. I hadn't looked at it. Now I look at my book every day.

A description of a character—This book has no characters. Well, again, that's a lie, because it has one character, the voice in my head, the voice who reads every word to me—Moses.

He was the kindest, funniest and funnest brother a girl could ever wish for. But he was unhappy. I didn't know. No one told me. He was ill, he was so unhappy. He was so unhappy that he couldn't find a way to live anymore. He couldn't find any way, except one way, the way out.

Who would I recommend the book to?—This is a book that makes me happier than any other; I just have to see it and I smile. But it is also a book that makes me sadder than any other. I wouldn't recommend this book to anyone. This is a book just for me.

I read my review in class. I read it fast. I read it without looking up from the page, crinkled and creased in front of me, my hands shaking.

It was hard at first. My voice was high and faltering. A tear, just one, escaped my eye. But then I steeled myself.

That's brilliant, isn't it? I steeled myself. I made myself into steel. Nothing could hurt me. I was cold and hard like metal.

Of course, I wasn't. Inside I shook and fluttered. I saw in my mind my class, friends and ex-friends alike, laughing and laughing. I saw Mr. Wills ripping up my report. I saw myself crumbling to dust.

But I held my voice steady. I stopped my hands shaking. I read word after word after word until they all flowed out, until everyone heard what I had not said before, what I'd never said, what had made me *the freak*.

And when I stopped no one laughed, no one spoke, no one even breathed.

I still did not look up from my page.

A sniff broke the silence, then a voice. "Thank you, Kaia," Mr. Wills said. "Thank you."

There was silence for a moment more and then

something I didn't expect—clapping. Not the riotous clapping of a class of eleven-year-olds, but a soft, gentle clapping. And it felt in that moment that they'd reserved this clap just for me.

I looked up.

I looked at Mr. Wills. He was dabbing his eye with a tissue.

I looked at the class, who looked at me, looked at me like I was something new, not something old and forgotten.

Then I looked at the boy. He was clapping with the rest, his head cocked to one side. And I knew he'd listened; every time, he'd listened.

I trembled and felt happy and scared and relieved all at once. I'd done it.

Soon, after a few more book reviews, real book reviews this time, it was break. We filed out of the classroom, heading for coats; the spring air still chilled us. Mr. Wills stopped me.

"Really, thank you," he said. And, "I'd love to see your book, Kaia. It means so much to you."

I nodded in reply and turned to leave but my teacher wasn't finished.

"And I'm sorry," Mr. Wills said. "I don't think I've always given you ... well ... enough time, I suppose."

I nodded again. I didn't know what to say. So I said nothing.

PINECONES

A crowd gathered round me. Most just said a word or two.

"That was amazing, Kaia."

"Sorry."

"Is the book here?"

Luzie and Angelica, Gemma and Hanaiya, made a wall around me; saved me again.

The boy was inside the wall. The boy was outside the wall. He danced in and out of the gathered faces. *He's lost in a crowd,* I thought.

It lasted a lifetime. It only lasted a minute or two. Eventually everyone found their game to play, friend to chase, ball to kick.

"That was really brave, Kai," Luzie said.

The other girls nodded.

I nodded.

"Thanks," I whispered. Something was stuck in my throat, something huge and spiky, a pinecone maybe.

"I need a drink," I said.

There's a bench by the water fountains. Not one of my favorites; it's always busy at the fountains. The boys use them as a safe house in tag. The girls gather by them to talk about the boys. Poppy must not know this, though.

She was sitting there. Alone. Her eyes were red, as if those cruel eyes had shed a tear.

I didn't make it to the fountains but stopped a few feet away, stuck, staring.

Poppy looked up. In her cool blue eyes I didn't see the usual hatred, the usual anger. For a moment she looked scared. For a moment she looked lost. She looked unsure of herself for the first time. Then she stood. And as she approached, her face changed, it hardened and Poppy was back.

The pinecone in my throat got bigger and bigger.

"You're still a freak to me," she spat.

The words hit me. Hard. The words pounded at my heart. But for all their crushing power, they didn't break through. And I knew then that the scars were healing. Damage was being undone. I knew then that I was ready.

In my mind my brother whispered once more.

"Let me go."

SUNFLOWER SEEDS

There are three words that ring through my mind as I set out for school the next morning.

"Let me go."

"Let me go."

"Let me go."

I see Mo in my mind, red and bloody. I see Mr. Wills drying his eyes. I see my class clapping. I see my mum's foul drink circling the drain. I see my friend, his deep gray eyes watching me, searching me, knowing me.

In my pocket, clutched in my sweaty hand, is a small white envelope.

I'm early. I know I'm early. I'm meeting someone. It's the best time to catch her. She's always at school early.

At the gates I have second thoughts. My hand tightens around the small packet. I don't want to let it go. For so long I've kept it close, kept it all close. I've locked it away, locked myself away.

I press my head against the cool, painted brick that forms the wall around our playground. I close my eyes.

"Let me go," Mo whispers.

Behind me I hear footsteps, light, cautious, but wild. I open my eyes to the boy. He's early too. And in that moment I love him more than ever. In that moment I need him more than ever.

He looks at me, considering, expectant.

"I'm ... I need to ..." I start but don't finish.

He cocks his head and smiles. A secret smile.

"Come on," I say. I can't speak the words, but I can show him, show him what I came to do.

We hold hands as we enter through the black

gates. He doesn't let go and neither do I as we circle the playground, checking amongst the flower beds for a telltale stripy sweater. I think she's not there until . . .

"Hello," Jo says.

I drop the boy's hand. I'm surprised, not embarrassed.

"Hello," I reply.

My friend stares. His seawater eyes absorbing the purple, green and orange of the gardener's knitted jumper.

Jo's carrying a tub, big and green, in both hands.

"It's a bit early to be here, isn't it?" she asks, then heaves the tub towards the nearest bed. Creeping vines stretch up and cover the wooden structure that shields the climbing frame. Jo makes our playground a jungle.

"I wanted . . . I need . . ."

The gardener puts down the tub. I see that it

is full of soft brown soil. I can smell its earthiness and I think that is how Jo must smell—earthy and real and deep.

She stares for a moment. "Maybe you could help me, Kaia? You can talk as we work," she says.

It's a simple job. We're refreshing the soil.

"Over time—and these creepers have been in for a good few years now—plants will take all the goodness out of the soil. You've got to give them fresh, new goodness to feed on. Most plants love a change," Jo says. "But you've got to do it carefully. Wait till they're ready. Give them time."

The boy doesn't help. He climbs and hangs and leaps around the frame. I watch him as I pat the warm earth.

"So," Jo says, the last fork of dirt applied. "How come you're here so early?"

I wipe my grubby hands on my jeans—they weren't that clean anyway. I reach into my pocket and pull out the envelope.

Two pairs of eyes are on me—the boy, perched

high in the vines; Jo, quiet, waiting—while I hold the package tight, almost to my mouth, then slowly, slowly, my arm like a growing branch, my hand unfurling like a spring bud, present it to the gardener.

She echoes my speed and takes it slowly. Slowly, slowly.

She opens it. My precious envelope.

"Sunflower seeds." She states this, then questions. "You want to plant them?"

I nod. And it's out, it's done. My breath, which I did not know I was holding, comes in one long draft. My heart pounds. I wipe a tear from my eye.

"We can do that, Kaia." Jo is nodding, smiling. "Maybe we could start a gardening club. Might have to talk to your teacher. You could talk to some of your friends. These could be our first project."

I nod. I smile. Then I grab Jo's big, woolly, stripy jumper and I squeeze her and I still haven't said a word.

"I'll take that as a yes," she says.

*   *   *

It was a week after the funeral.

I was sitting alone. It felt like I had not been alone for a long time, so many people in and out. But even in the middle of all that I still felt like I was all alone in the world. Moses was gone.

I sat on the floor, in front of my mirror. I was counting the freckles speckled across my nose. They made me think of glitter. Mum did not have freckles. Moses did not have freckles, had not had freckles. It was where I saw a dad I'd never met, right there in my freckles, a dad who lived in some distant land with a family of his own.

Behind me, in the reflection, my bookcase called to me. Freckle counting could only draw me away from the pain for moments. Could I escape into a book?

I stood and flicked through my stories. No cover held me, none of those shiny pink ones that I had loved. Then I saw it, the corner peeking out from beneath my bed—*Trees of Britain: An Illustrated Guide.*

Kneeling as if in prayer, I laid the book like something sacred on my duvet. I ran my hand across the cover. I ran a finger along the unbroken spine.

As the fresh tears fell I whispered, "Sorry, Mo," and opened my birthday present. I had thanked him for it on the day and kissed his stubbly cheek but then the bike appeared and my book lay forgotten.

I flicked through the pages, offering a tear to each leaf. I flicked till I found the reason for my brother's question—"Are you enjoying the book?"

There, beneath the illustration of a cherry tree in blossom, was hidden a handwritten note. Beside this, a small white envelope.

Dearest Tiny,

Happy birthday, little one. You're getting so old. You're like an old, old lady. Soon your hair will be turning gray and you'll be hobbling to school.

I've thought of a well good project for us to do before your knees give out and your back's too weak. Let's plant a garden! It's pretty rough, our patch of grass and few old bushes. Mum says we can do it.

Pick a tree you'd like, there's a garden center just near your school that does baby trees. Here's a packet of seeds to get us started. They're sunflowers, like my sunny, fluffy-headed, tiny sister.

Have a good, good day.

Big Love,
Your brother, Mo

Rule for Life

Plant a seed.

HAPPINESS

My mum got the job. She got the job. And as far as I can tell, she hasn't touched a bottle since she poured all that horrible drink down our sink.

Actually, she has touched a bottle—we had Chinese food to celebrate Mum's job and it came with a big bottle of Coke. We had chicken in black bean sauce, sweet and sour pork, rice and prawn crackers. I felt a bit strange eating it; Chinese food was always Mo's favorite. I don't think Mum even thought about that, though. She got the job.

This all happened; then cycle training started. It is as brilliant as I hoped. No Mr. Wills, fresh spring air, time with my friend, and maybe, maybe some new friends.

Our instructors are pretty good too.

Ben's in charge and he's got a beard. That makes him sound old. He's not. He's really young. Young compared to all the teachers, anyway. But he's got a beard. Beards are usually reserved for old people; granddads have beards, not young cycling instructors. Anyway, he does have a beard. The boy kept pointing and growling. Don't ask me why. Maybe he'd never seen a beard before.

Mary's young too. She really likes my bike. I told her that my brother painted it for me. She said that I was really lucky to have such a fantastic big brother. I didn't tell her that I don't have a big brother. Luzie touched me on the arm after Mary started talking about something else. And somehow this touch made my heart unclench and my breath come easy.

Yes, I had friends.

We'd done all the basics. They checked that we could, well, cycle in a straight line. Then they taught us how to turn corners safely, where to position ourselves on the road, what to do at traffic lights and all that stuff.

We cheered each other when we got things right and we laughed at each other when we did something daft. The laughing was almost as good as the cheering. I don't know why.

Ben tried to teach me to look backwards. I couldn't get the hang of it. I looked over my left shoulder, then my right, then my left again. By this point I was going so slowly that the bike just stopped and I tumbled to the ground. Shadid and Deon were even quicker than the boy at coming to help me up.

Once I'd brushed myself down, Luzie called out, "You're such a dappy one, Kaia."

Angelica did a mime of me looking one way, then the other, then the other, over and over again. We only stopped laughing when Mary started shouting at us to take it seriously.

Most days we've had break and lunchtime with the rest of the school. But today we started going out on the road. Our cycle went over break time but no one minded, not even Shadid and Deon, who usually spend every break time playing football or pat-ball.

When we stopped for our own break, we rested the bikes against a wall and stood in a circle. Mary handed out little bottles of water from her rucksack and we all chatted. We chatted about TV mostly. I didn't have much to say.

It was wonderful.

COLLISION

On the last day of cycle training, spring was in full bloom. The daffs were everywhere. Along the road, outside school, pink blossoms coated the cherry trees (*Prunus serrulata*), which when in bloom are the most beautiful trees around.

The cherry is awash with color throughout the year, with coppery brown– to bronze-colored leaves throughout the autumn and even into spring, and vivid purplish-pink double flowers opening from crimson buds.

I can say, I think with certainty, that it was the happiest I'd been since ... well, you know.

I think with certainty—but that means I'm not certain. Let's change that.

I'm fairly sure that it was the happiest I'd been. Now that sounds stupid.

I was happy. Let's leave it at that.

Spring. Friends. Mum. I was happy.

"Today, we're gonna see what you've learned," Ben said, first thing. "We're going on a ride, further than we've been before. You'll need to show us all your new skills."

"We'll be watching all the time," Mary added.

But they weren't, were they? If they were ... well, if they were, it wouldn't have happened. Not that I blame them at all. No, I blame me.

We'd cycled for maybe fifteen minutes and we were already further than we'd been before. Ben and Mary had been cycling in amongst us, encouraging, reminding us of what we'd learned.

"I can see you've remembered to look behind you, Luz."

"Make sure you indicate, Shadid. Put your hand out, that's it."

"Yes, excellent, a good straight line, Kaia."

I was beaming.

Now we'd hit a hill, not the steepest, but certainly the longest of the day. And little by little, bit by bit, they were pulling away.

"Come on, slow-coaches. Keep on pedaling," Ben called as he glanced back along the line.

I was at the back with the boy; Luzie a little way in front. Under my thin T-shirt and baggy jumper I could feel droplets of sweat tickling their way down my spine. Ahead, my friends were standing on their pedals, pushing down, shooting forwards, little spurts of speed. I was steady, sitting in a low gear.

Gradually the instructors got further and further away. Cars didn't pull round us as a group now; they went round me and the boy, then in, then round Luzie, then in, then round the rest.

As we reached the top of the hill, the road split. To the right, where Mary and Ben continued, the road flattened with houses on either side. To the left, the long height we'd just climbed slid down, much steeper than the road we'd taken. Off past the steep descent, over the roofs and chimneys of lined-up homes, a sea of green appeared—trees and trees, unidentifiable at that distance. The sea of Giant Park.

I stopped to see the view and catch my breath. The boy stopped, his feet hitting the tarmac heavily. A car swung round us, the driver beeping his horn. We shuffled closer to the curb.

The boy eyed the hill, his eyes flashing. I eyed the boy.

"Shall we?" I asked.

The boy eyed me, glinting gray piercing.

"OK." I grinned, pushing away from the tarmac, heading left.

We picked up speed quickly, no matter how I squeezed the brakes. The boy giggled and I gasped. It was scary. It was exciting. It was wild.

Parked cars flashed past, green, blue, white, white, red, yellow, blue, green, red, red, red, red.

My helmet slipped backwards. I reached up to reposition it. It felt flimsy compared to the power of our descent.

The bottom of the hill rushed up to meet us: a crossing, some shops, traffic lights.

Traffic lights on green.

Traffic lights turning amber.

I squeezed both brakes. They squealed. I slowed, a little, but not enough.

The boy was no longer laughing; he tried to place his odd-shod feet on the ground, tried to stop. Brakes squealed.

Traffic lights turned red.

We careered forwards.

I see it coming. I think I see it coming. From the right, red, blood red, filled my vision.

I heard it. A third set of brakes squealed. A horn blasted. The boy shouted.

I feel it. Air driven from my lungs. Pain beyond feeling.

Then nothing.

Nothing.

Darkness.

Rule for Life

When you're on the right track,

don't take a wrong turn.

GOODBYES

Darkness for a long time. Dark and cold. I heard voices.

"Broken," they'd say.

"Lost blood."

"Too much damage."

Tears I heard too, muffled, as if from behind a thick curtain.

"Kaia."

"My Kaia."

"Please wake up."

But mostly it was dark, dark and cold.

Then it was light. Not the light of the waking world. A light all around, coming from everywhere, and I wasn't there, but I was there. And there was Moses and he was there. No cap on this time, eyes alight with a secret smile.

"Well, that was stupid, wasn't it, Tiny?" he said.

I laugh, but I don't laugh because I'm not there, not really.

Now, looking back, I know that I should have been wondering if I was dead. But I wasn't thinking that at all. I wasn't thinking at all.

"You know what I need to say, don't you?" the angel Moses said. And I *did* know.

"Well, goodbye, then," he says.

"Goodbye," I say inside.

Then it's dark again.

I woke up today. Warmth first, then light, real light this time.

Have you ever woken up and just felt so hungry that you're not sure you'll even make it to the kitchen before you collapse and are forced to eat your own arm? No, perhaps not that hungry. Anyway, as hungry as you've ever been, I was hungrier. I felt like someone had removed my stomach. I just had an empty space where it should be.

There was no food around when I awoke and no people either. I was in a white room, white walls, white window frames, white ceiling, white sheets on my bed, firmly tucking me in. The door was blue, though, and the floor speckled blue linoleum. And one wall was covered in a multicolored array of cards, some shop-bought, most hand-drawn, which I assumed must have belonged to the person who slept here before me. I certainly didn't have that many friends.

To my right was a machine, which gently bleeped away; to my left a metal stand with a bag hanging from it. Both of these had tubes or wires connecting them to my body, one up my nose, one into my wrist, several stuck to my chest.

My body, my body, the crash came flooding back to me: red, blood, blood, red. My body didn't feel too bad. My right arm was set in a cast. I could feel bandages wrapped around my chest. My face felt tight, almost rigid. But apart from that, I felt all right.

I knew it must be a hospital room, I'd seen enough on TV. Even though my hunger was crippling I didn't call for a nurse, not right away, at least. I stared out the window.

I could only see sky, blue, blue sky, washed in a few places with a wisp of white cloud. High above, a lone gray gull squawked and carried on its way, down to the river, then out to sea. I could have kept staring into that blue abyss but my door opened with a sigh and in came a large, singing woman.

"When we've been there ten thousand years, bright shining as the sun," she sang as she backed into the room, her backside wiggling.

The bucket she wheeled in told me that she was a cleaner. She began another line, "We've no less days … ," then turned and saw me staring.

"Hello," I said.

"Oh, sweetheart, hello," she said, then straight-away, "I'll get the nurse."

"Wait!" I called out, but I was too slow; she was gone. I stared out the window again but the gull did not return.

"She can't be awake, Janelli." A voice drifted down the corridor towards me, followed by a tired and pregnant nurse.

"Hello," I said again.

"Oh my word!" the nurse exclaimed, then quickly, "I'll get the doctor."

My "Wait!" was too slow again and I watched both the cleaner and the nurse rush from the room.

I had a little longer to stare out into the world this time, and I found myself thinking about the boy. He must, I thought, be just next door, or at least on the same ward. With this thought I decided not to wait for the doctor and slipped out from under the sheets. Then I did what on reflection I can see was another stupid thing: I pulled the wires off my chest and the tubes out of my nose and arm. Instantly the machine let out a constant beep and the tube that had been in my arm leaked a clear liquid onto the bed. Like I said, I felt all right.

I was wearing my own pajamas, and in a tall, thin cupboard I found my own dressing gown, a hand-me-down from Moses. I sniffed it, as I always did, hoping to catch a long-lost scent of my brother like a message from the past in nasal form.

It's strange finding something you own somewhere you've never seen it before; you know someone's tampered with it, rifled through your belongings. I stuck my hands into the threadbare pockets. Something dry and crisp and rough tickled the fingers of my left hand.

Just then, giving me no time to glance at the mystery object, the doctor appeared.

"Hello," I said for a third time.

"Hello," said the doctor, a beautiful woman. I could not say whether she was young or old. She wasn't black or white either; her skin was a dark hazelnut. "I'm Dr. Sanogo," she went on. "I am one of your doctors, Kaia." I had *doctors*, not just *a* doctor. "Can I just check you over quickly?"

I nodded and Dr. Sanogo nodded. Her big frizzy hair tied up above her head nodded too.

"And I think Laura here"—indicating the nurse, who had returned without the cleaner—"better get you plugged back in."

While the nurse eased me back into bed, Dr. Sanogo did her checks. She held my wrist and felt my pulse. She took my temperature. She asked me a few questions, like my name, my mum's name, my date of birth. I think I got them all right.

When she was done, she turned to the nurse, who was long finished and had been hovering nervously by the door. "Laura," the doctor said, "have you called Kaia's mum?"

"I thought I'd better wait," she replied.

"Well, that's the first thing to do now." The

nurse left. "Second," the doctor went on, "I'd better get you something to eat. You must be starving."

She turned to leave, but I was quicker this time. "Wait," I said, and my doctor turned back towards me. "Please, Doctor, where is the boy?"

"Boy?" the doctor replied.

"The boy. My friend."

She stared at me blankly and I started to panic, my breath coming in short spurts and the machines beeping, getting faster and faster.

"The boy," I tried again. "He would have arrived with me. He was in the crash too."

The doctor stared some more; then, when she began to speak she did so slowly, like I was madder than I knew I was. "You arrived on your own, Kaia. There was no one else in the crash. Do you mean the driver? He wasn't hurt."

My eyes were filled with tears now. "Not the driver," I said. "The boy, the boy."

The doctor took a step back towards me, placing her hand on my shoulder. "I'm going to see about that food. Then I think we'd better do a few more checks, sweetheart."

I didn't reply but watched the doctor disappear through the door.

I sat stunned for some time, possibilities racing through my head. Then I remembered the something rough lodged in my pocket. It rasped against my dressing gown as I pulled it out and brought it up to my face.

A long, green-brown horse chestnut leaf. I saw him then, my boy, a smiling face, deep gray eyes, hair as black as coal. The world spun around him.

Summer had almost arrived when he left. I had been asleep, "in a coma," the doctor said, for four weeks. And in that time a warm breeze had crept in to replace the spring rain and remove any doubt that the frost was over. The boy had left. I asked after him one last time. I asked my mum, but she stared at me as blankly as the doctors.

"Oh, my Kaia" were her first words when she

walked in yesterday, the day I woke up. "I'm so sorry I wasn't here."

I looked her up and down. She was wearing a white shirt and a green vest over the top. Pinned to the vest was a name badge, her name badge. It looked distinctly like a uniform.

"You've started your job, Mum," I said.

We grinned at each other for a long time. Then hugged for a long time. I cried and laughed and we hugged some more, me and my mum.

"I'm sorry, Kaia," my mum whispered again and again into the top of my hair, and I knew that she meant it. I knew she meant it for everything. I was sorry too.

When we finally let go of each other, Mum took hold of my hands and kissed my forehead.

"Have you seen all your cards, Kaia?" she said.

I looked back at the wall, covered in cards. "*My* cards?" I said.

"I didn't know you were such a popular girl, sweetheart."

I didn't know I was such a popular girl.

"Some of your friends have been in so many times, bringing you all sorts of things. Luzie and Angelica and a boy." At this my mum winked at me. "Shadid."

I found myself blushing.

My mum leaned across me, behind the metal stand (an IV drip, I now know), to a bedside cabinet. She opened the top drawer. It was stuffed with books, bags of sweets, pencils and paper, and on top, Luzie's magnet game.

"Some teachers came too—Mr. Wills came on the first day; Harry came, he brought you these paints." Mum held up a tin of watercolor paints, a pad and paintbrush. "Jo's been a few times, been telling you about some sunflowers she's planted for you, getting big, she says."

Again my eyes filled with tears and I thought of the boy, my boy, who had made all this possible.

Rule for Life

Everything changes.

THE END

Through the open window, summer sunlight slants into the room and I hear the call of a distant bird, nesting high in the welcoming arms of an ancient sycamore (*Acer pseudoplatanus*). I realize that it is far too warm for the blankets that lie across my legs. Before I shift them my eye catches, again, the slender leaf, pinned with my many cards against the wall. For one last time I whisper to the boy, with a secret smile, "Goodbye, friend."

My mum walks in, her uniform creased. She smiles at me, her eyes aglow. I stare at her. She stares at me.

"You have such a lovely smile, Kaia," she says.

ACKNOWLEDGMENTS

In all things, my first and highest thanks go to God, whose goodness towards me knows no bounds.

Many people read this book before it got to "official" hands. Chief amongst them were a group of children who read every word I wrote, even the ones that didn't make the cut. Special thanks to O.C.—I want to see you writing one day.

Thanks go to: Jonny Stockwood, a fellow writer—your advice is always invaluable; Maggie and Laurie—you always believe in my scribblings; Simon Tarry—you're the most supportive guy I know.

When the manuscript for this book found its way into the hands of professionals, Penny Holroyde, my agent, believed in and championed me, Kaia and the boy right from the start. The team at Andersen, Eloise and Charlie and Ruth, took it and helped me shape it and made it more beautiful with their insightful ideas, always presented with gentleness—thank you. A massive glug of thanks goes to Kate, whose incredible illustration graces the cover of this book.

A last thanks, but certainly not the least, goes to my wife. Chloe, you are a woman of infinite patience, trust and love. This book would not exist without you.

Tom Avery is the author of the middle-grade novel *Too Much Trouble*, winner of the Frances Lincoln Diverse Voices Children's Book Award. He was born and raised in London in a very large, very loud family, descendants of the notorious pirate Henry Avery. Tom has worked as a teacher in inner-city schools in London and Birmingham. He lives in North London with his wife and two sons.